SCELIDOSAURUS

(ske-LIE-duh-SAW-rus)

TYRANNOSAURUS

(tie-RAN-uh-SAW-rus)

TRICERATOPS

(try-SER-uh-tops)

STEGOSAURUS

(STEG-uh-SAW-rus)

PTERODACTYL

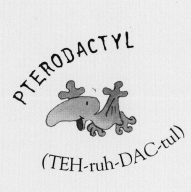

(TEH-ruh-DAC-tul)

APATOSAURUS

(uh-PAT-uh-SAW-rus)

ANCHISAURUS

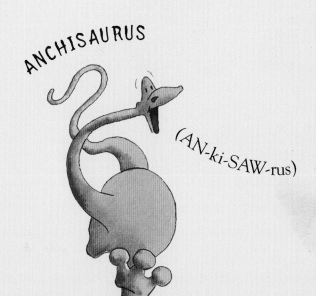

(AN-ki-SAW-rus)

For Matthew Edward Traynor
—I.W.

For Aonghas and Mairead
—A.R.

Text copyright © 2004 by Ian Whybrow
Illustrations copyright © 2004 by Adrian Reynolds
All rights reserved under International and Pan-American Copyright Conventions.
Published in the United States by Random House Children's Books, a division of
Random House, Inc., New York.
First published in 2004 by Puffin Books, a division of the Penguin Group,
80 Strand, London, WC2R 0RL, England.
www.randomhouse.com/kids

Library of Congress Cataloging-in-Publication Data
Whybrow, Ian. Harry and the dinosaurs at the museum /
by Ian Whybrow; illustrated by Adrian Reynolds. — 1st American ed.
p. cm.
SUMMARY: When his family goes to a museum so that big sister Sam can research human
ancestors, young Harry wanders off while playing with his toy dinosaurs and becomes lost,
but Gran knows just where to find him.
ISBN 0-375-83338-2 (trade)
[1. Museums—Fiction. 2. Dinosaurs—Fiction. 3. Lost children—Fiction. 4. Toys—Fiction.]
I. Reynolds, Adrian, ill. II. Title.
PZ7.W6225Hann 2005 [E]—dc22
2004018888
MANUFACTURED IN CHINA First American Edition 2005 10 9 8 7 6 5 4 3 2 1
RANDOM HOUSE and colophon are registered trademarks of Random House, Inc.

Harry and the Dinosaurs at the Museum

Ian Whybrow and Adrian Reynolds

Random House 🏠 New York

Sam wanted Mom to take her to the museum.
She had to study the Romans for homework.
"What are Romans?" asked Harry.

Sam said they were our ancestors, but he was
too young to understand.
Harry wanted to take the dinosaurs to see them.

Sam said, "No way!"
She said Harry would just get bored and silly.
That was why Sam's homework got smudged.

Mom made them both settle down.
She said a museum would be a fine
outing for everybody.
"I'd love to go," said Gran.

The museum was bigger than a hospital.
You had to have a map.

On the way to the Romans, they passed the cavemen.
"Are these ancestors?" asked Harry.

Mom said yes, everybody in the world came from cavemen. They lit fires and hunted.

Harry liked the stone axes.

The dinosaurs liked the saber-toothed tiger!
"Raahh! Sharp teeth!"

Next stop was the Egyptians.

They saw mummies in boxes and funny writing like pictures.

"Are Egyptians ancestors?" asked Harry.

"Yes, but not the right ones," said Sam. "We want the Romans. Come on, hurry up!"

Finally they reached the Romans.
They had big swords and spears, and
helmets with brushes on them.

But what a lot of old pots, broken ones, too!
Sam started drawing.
"We've seen the Romans now," said Harry.
"I'm hungry! Let's go!"

"Raahh! Anchisaurus pinched me!" said Stegosaurus.
"He's taking up all the room!" said Anchisaurus.
"Behave!" said Harry in a loud voice.
"Look, Harry *is* being silly!" groaned Sam. "I knew it!"

"I think the dinosaurs need to run around a little," said Harry.

Mom said better not. They might get lost.

"Come on, let's get something to eat," she said.

"Afterward we'll come back here so Sam can finish her research."

The cafeteria was very busy. Gran and Harry and the dinosaurs saved a table while Mom and Sam stood in line.

"Look, I'm a caveman! Raahh!" said Triceratops.
"Look, I'm a Roman! Raahh!" said Pterodactyl.
"Look, I'm a mummy! Raahh!" said Tyrannosaurus.

After lunch, everyone felt a lot better and they
set off back to the Romans.
But it wasn't long before Anchisaurus got bored.
"I'm bored, too!" said Tyrannosaurus.

"Never mind," said Harry. "It's your turn to do some studying. Pay attention, my dinosaurs."
He taught them Climbing up Display Cases.
Then he taught them Sliding on the Slippery Floor.

That was how they got lost.

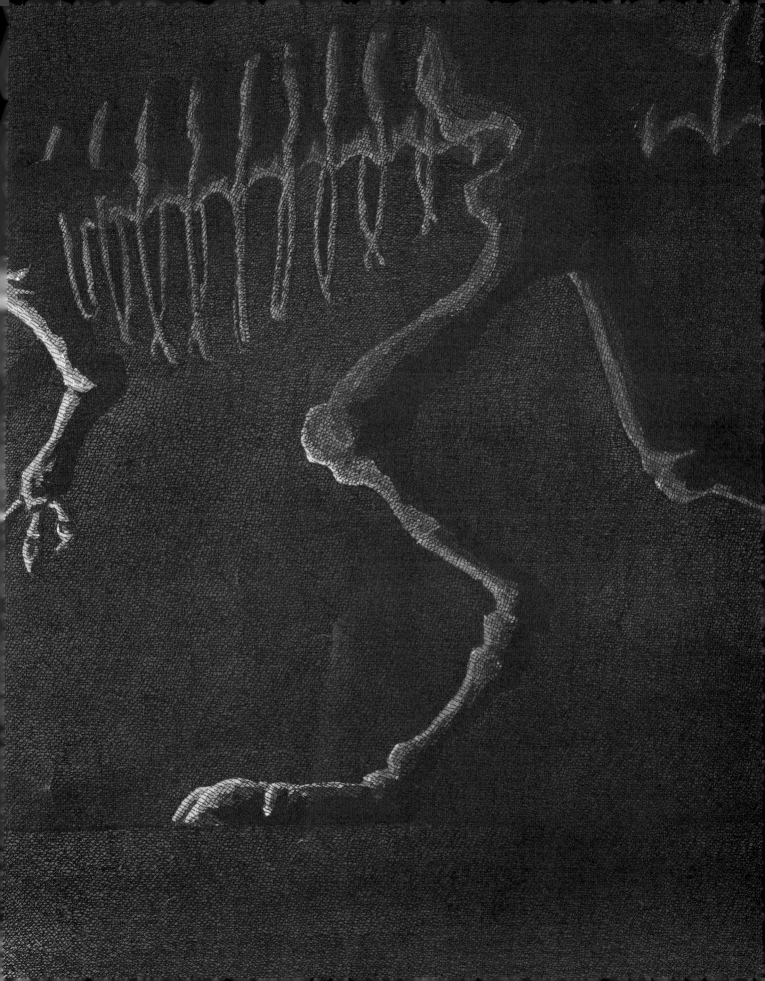

"Oh no! Where's Harry?" said Mom.
"Quick! Let's find the person in charge!"
"I just *knew* he'd get lost," said Sam.
"Nonsense!" said Gran. "I bet I know
where we'll find him!"

They followed Gran to the Prehistoric Hall.
"There he is," said Gran. "I knew it."

Harry was still teaching his dinosaurs.
"Boys come from cavemen and Romans and Egyptians,"
he explained. "But these are *your* ancestors."

So Tyrannosaurus said, "Raahh!" to his ancestor.
So did Apatosaurus and Scelidosaurus and Triceratops
and the rest of the bucketful of dinosaurs.
All except Pterodactyl, who gave his ancestor a nose-rub.

"Now, young man!" said the person in charge.
"We had better look for your mother. Could you
tell me your name?"

Harry said his name, address, and telephone number,
no problem at all.
All the people said Harry was a very good, clever boy.
"He's with us!" called Gran proudly, rushing over.

"Harry!" said Mom. "We thought we'd lost you!"

"I wasn't lost!" said Harry. "I was with my dinosaurs."

"And we were with our ancestors," said the dinosaurs. "RAAAHH!"
ENDOSAURUS

SCELIDOSAURUS

(ske-LIE-duh-SAW-rus)

TYRANNOSAURUS

(tie-RAN-uh-SAW-rus)

WITHDRAWN

TRICERATOPS

(try-SER-uh-tops)

STEGOSAURUS

(STEG-uh-SAW-rus)

PTERODACTYL

(TEH-ruh-DAC-tul)

APATOSAURUS

(uh-PAT-uh-SAW-rus)

ANCHISAURUS

(AN-ki-SAW-rus)